# CODE RACERS

Adapted by Mary Man-Kong
Based on the screenplay by Nina Bargiel with additional writing by Jennifer Skelly
Cover illustrated by Elisabetta Melaranci, Patrizia Zangrilli, and Ann Beliashova
Interiors illustrated by Elisabetta Melaranci, Federica Salfo, and Francesco Legramandi

Special thanks to Ryan Ferguson, Debra Mostow Zakarin, Sammie Suchland, Kristine Lombardi, Nicole Corse, Karen Painter, Stuart Smith, Charnita Belcher, Julia Phelps, Julia Pistor, Renata Marchand, Garrett Sander, Kris Fogel, Rachael Datello, Michael Goguen, Lauren Rose, Sarah Serata, and Rainmaker Entertainment

## A RANDOM HOUSE PICTUREBACK® BOOK

## RANDOM HOUSE 🏠 NEW YORK

Published in the United States by Random House Children's Books, a division of Penguin Random House LLC, 1745 Broadway, New York, NY 10019, and in Canada by Penguin Random House Canada Limited, Toronto. No part of this book may be reproduced or copied in any form without written permission from the copyright owner. Pictureback, Random House, and the Random House colophon are registered trademarks of Penguin Random House LLC.
ISBN 978-0-399-55932-7
randomhousekids.com   Printed in the United States of America   10 9 8 7 6 5 4 3 2

One day, Barbie was playing her favorite video game, *Cupcake Caverns,* with her friends Renee and Teresa. Barbie made an advanced move as she opened a coding window and created a special flying power-up. They were about to win when Renee's flying llama was hit by a cupcake. GAME OVER!

Before signing off, Renee asked how Barbie's dance audition had gone.

"I thought the eighth time was the charm," said Barbie, "but I didn't make it."

Unfortunately, the teacher didn't appreciate Barbie's unique dance moves.

Later that day, a cute character popped up on Barbie's tablet. It invited her to test a new game. When Barbie tapped yes, thousands of bubbles came out of the screen. They surrounded her and pulled her into the tablet!

Barbie soon found herself *inside* the video game!

The cute character said, "I wish to be no stranger. I'm known as Cutie, and our world is in danger!"

Cutie, the in-game tutorial, said an Emoji virus had infected the game. Cutie knew Barbie was one of the top video game players. If Barbie could win every level, the virus would be defeated.

"Let's play!" said Barbie.

In Level One, Barbie met her opponents, Bella and Kris.
"Look, Kris, a newbie," called Bella.
"Don't worry," said Barbie. "I can skate."
Bella and Kris dodged every obstacle and zoomed ahead.
Barbie jumped onto a glowing surfboard. It was a
power-up! Soon she caught up with Bella and Kris.

Suddenly, the Emoji virus attacked a Ferris wheel, which began to roll toward them.

Barbie snagged another power-up and grabbed hold of Bella and Kris. She knew she couldn't leave them behind.

Bella and Kris didn't understand why Barbie was helping them.

Barbie explained that she had to win every level to beat the virus. Bella and Kris agreed to work with Barbie as a team. They all raced together, and at the finish line, Bella and Kris pushed Barbie ahead.

"Winner: Barbie!" said the game voice.

Barbie got her first trophy: a star made from blocks of code. She realized she could use the code to create almost anything!

In Level Two, Barbie and her friends were transformed into 2-D stickers! They saw nutty squirrels throwing acorns at a tree house. Crystal, who lived in the tree house, needed their help. She told them that to win the game, players had to match crystals to bring the tree house safely down to the ground.

© Mattel

With Barbie's encouragement, Kris and Bella worked together to block the acorns from destroying the tree so Barbie could match the crystals. Kris and Bella were learning how to be part of a team.

"Winner: Barbie!" announced the game voice.

But they had no time to waste. The Emoji virus and the squirrels were overrunning the level! Luckily, Crystal had a special car, and the players escaped through a waterfall.

While picking up her next star trophy, Barbie noticed a portal and jumped through it.

It was a bonus level! Two sisters, Gaia and Maia, were lined up to race against Barbie.

Barbie explained that she needed to beat the level to defeat the Emoji virus. Maia and Gaia understood, but there was a problem. "We can't slow down!" said Gaia.

Barbie did her best, but the sisters were too fast.

"Winner: Maia!" declared the game voice.

Barbie felt terrible that she hadn't saved their level from the Emoji virus.

"It's not your fault, it's mine," said Cutie. He admitted that he had been lonely and wanted to create some new friends. But he had messed up the coding and produced the Emoji virus instead!

Fortunately, Barbie didn't need to win the bonus level to win the game.

Barbie and Cutie rejoined their friends in Level Three, which transformed them into pixels. Barbie wasn't sure she'd be able to defeat the virus.

"I didn't bring you here to beat the game," said Cutie. "I brought you here to change it."

Barbie realized she could use her imagination to change the game! She built a portal with the other pixel blocks. "I'll be right back!" she said as she jumped inside.

Barbie went back to the bonus level to rerun the race against Gaia and Maia. This time, she used new code to make her own bridge to pass them.

Barbie swerved to miss hitting the Emoji virus and clung to the side of a cliff! Luckily, Bella had followed her to the bonus level and helped her up.

Barbie blasted over the finish line—one step ahead of the Emoji virus!

"Winner: Barbie!" said the game voice.

Barbie and Bella returned to Level Three. The Emoji virus chased the players through the level.

Kris found a cupcake power-up and picked up a Cupcake Blaster. He slowed down the virus, giving Barbie time to open a code window.

Barbie opened her inventory bag, which was filled with code stars. There had to be a way to stop the virus!

Bella had an idea. With a few changes to the code, they loaded the code stars into the Cupcake Blaster—and created an antivirus!

"Hey, virus breath, over here!" teased Bella. She and Kris darted
back and forth, luring the virus closer to Barbie until it was in range.
Barbie cornered the Emoji virus and activated the Cupcake Blaster.
The virus was destroyed, and the level was won!

But then pieces of the Emoji virus came back together. It was forming a giant super virus! Barbie and her friends didn't know what to do.

"Games are supposed to be fun," Bella said. "Why bother saving a game that isn't?"

Barbie knew it was time to change the game and make it fun again. She used her final pieces of game code. In a shower of glitter, the code created an amazing dance floor!

"Welcome to the final level!" said the game voice.

The dance moves were difficult to execute in pixel form, so Barbie changed the code so she was back to her original form. Then she danced in her own unique way to gain all the points. Everyone joined in!

The score went back and forth, but soon, Barbie was surging ahead. Happy emojis started to fall off the virus.

Barbie's plan worked! With the help of her friends, the super virus was defeated and the game was saved!

A glowing trophy dropped from the clouds.

"Remember, creating your own path is not just for this space," said Cutie. "You can take this talent to any old place."

"Thank you," said Barbie.

Finally, Barbie gave her last bit of code to one of the happy emojis. Instantly, an invitation to play popped up on screens around the world.

"It's now a multiplayer game," Barbie told Cutie. "You'll never be lonely again!"

Then a code tornado came to take Barbie home.

"Bye, everyone," Barbie called. "Good game!"

When Barbie returned to her room, she saw her sister Chelsea dancing to something on her tablet.

"Barbie, I'm sorry you didn't make the honors dance team, but I found this awesome dance game that we can play together," said Chelsea.

"Actually, I've been thinking of putting together my own dance team," said Barbie.

"Can you do that?" asked Chelsea.

"Of course. You can always create your own path," Barbie replied with a wink.